THE STRENGTH

IN OUR SCARS

Written And Illustrated

By NATHAN RYAN

Dedicated to Dr Rob and Anne. Thanks for all the love and care.

Not too long ago in a magical place not too far from here, a tiger and his one true love lived. Their days were filled with joy and passion and they were very happy.

Soon a beautiful cub was born and enriched their lives. They were overjoyed and their family was complete. They called him Seven or Sev for short. They believed in happily ever after.

Then a little while later Sev was very sick. So they went to the Children's Hospital where he met an amazing man named Docor Rob. Doctor Rob took very good care of Sev and he was wonderful and very caring. Sev was born with so much love and light in his heart that he shone brighter than the stars. His heart was so full of rays of sunshine that it broke. He needed surgery. Sev was very brave and with Doctor Rob's except help and care, Sev got well.

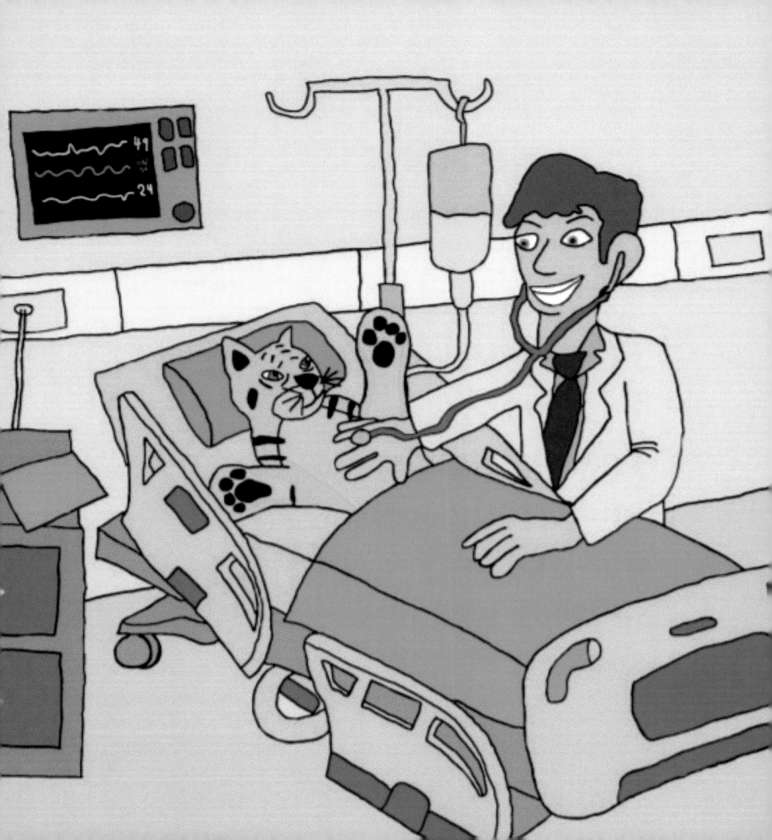

The little cub needed heart surgery. After surgery, his heart was better. It was beating steady and strong. Sev got well very quickly and soon went home.

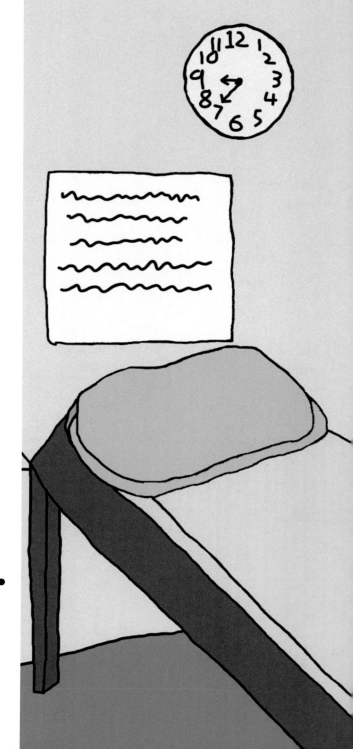

Many years later the little cub was stronge and well. Sev was so full of energy. He did lots of exercise to stay strong. Sev felt the low hum of possibility in the centre of his chest and that enthralled him. He felt alive and powerful in his heart. He felt capable with infinite possibilities. He knew he was loved and he could succeed at anything. One day Sev went walking in the jungle. He passed a cheeky monkey in a tree.

The monkey said "Hello and they started to talk. "Where are you going?" asked the monkey. Sev said "I am going for a walk to the river." The monkey then noticed the scar on Sev's chest. "You have a zipper on your chest, the lion will eat you."

The monkey started to laugh. He laughed so hard he fell out of the tree. Sev ignored him and kept walking.

A little further up the path he saw a peacock. "Hello" the cub said with a big smile.

"Hi there" said the peacock. "Don't pay any attention to the monkey. He is always rude. I heard what he said to you and I'am glad you ignored him. He told me I was ugly." "You are beautiful" said Sev. The peacock smiled and then he strutted his tail feathers and said "I like who I am." He walked away.

Sev could see the river. He jumped onto a log and was surprised to see a crocodile getting some sun at the edge of the water. "Hello! Great day isn't it?" Sev said with a smile. They chatted for a while. Then the crocodile asked Sev about his scar." It is an ugly scar from surgery," he told his new friend. The crocodile said, "No it isn't. What I see is not what you think. What I see is the pain you went through and the strength inside you. The scars don't beat you down. They are a physical reminder and a map of how brave you are and your strength and courage." Sev thought about his words. He looked closer at the crocodile and realised the he had some scars too. The crocodile flicked his tail and swam away.

Sev continued his walk until he saw an elephant. They talked and laughed.

Sev watched the ripples in the water.

The elephant stared for a long time. Then he asked, "Why do you have a scar?" Sev answered, "it is my battle scar." The elephant was quiet for a long time.

"Look at your reflection in the water." Sev sat at the edge on the rocks and was surprised to see he had a Medal of Honor for bravery on his chest and a crown for courage on his head.

Lurking in the jungle behind Sev, was a lion watching patiently. He was waiting for lunch.

The elephant then bellowed with laughter. Leo the lion is the King of the Jungle. He jumped in fright from behind you in the trees when he saw you and your reflection he got scared of your strength. Looks like he has made you a new superhero and King of the Jungle."

Sev continued walking and ran into a Phoenix. The bird said he had healing powers and could heal the scar." Sev said, "No thanks, I fought for my life and my scar is apart of my journey. I am happy and strong with lots of love in my heart."

They talked for a long and Sev continued his walk with his new friend for a while.

Sev came to a mountain. A long climb inspired by the idea of a new challenge and the reward of a great view at the top. Sun poured through the trees casting him in yellow light. It made his green eyes shine bright. He thought to himself, "Life is about chasing dreams and living in awe of your own strength." Eyes wide with hope and enjoyment. "I am in charge of my own life. I know for certain I will count each day and memory to the fullest."

Sev wore his scar with pride. He was confident and unafraid.

His heart and soul were living in the moment and he lived happily ever after.

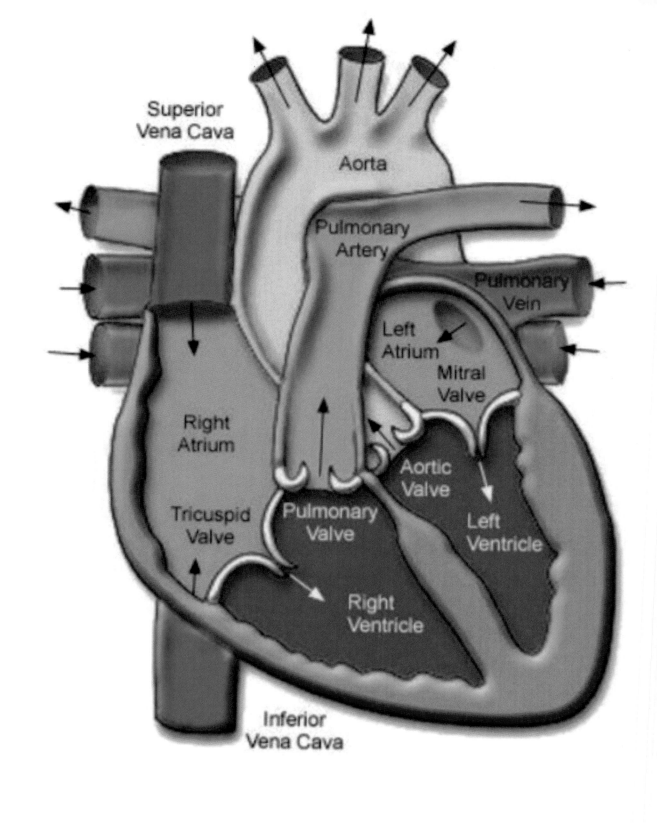

A scar is a gift -

Strength

Courage

Achieve

Resilience

Made in the USA
Middletown, DE
02 November 2020